GARBAGE!

The Trashiest Book You'll Ever Read

SUZANNE LORD

SCHOLASTIC INC.
New York Toronto London Auckland Sydney

PHOTO CREDITS

Black-and-white interior photos:

1990 TBS Productions, Inc., CHARACTERS 1990 TBS Productions, Inc. and DIC Enterprises, Inc.: p. 99; AP/Wide World Photos: p. 26; AP Laser Photo/Adam Stoltman: p. 23; AP Laser Photo/John Gaps III: p. 25; AP Laser Photo/Michel Lipchitz: p. 27; Eric Kroll: p. 5; Four By Five: p. 9; Gene Breckner/Valley Press: p. 87; German Information Center: p. 78; Leo de Wys Inc./Bill Bachman: p. 61; Leo de Wys Inc./Danilo Buschung: p. 13; Leo de Wys Inc. David Lissy: p. 49; Leo de Wys Inc./George Munday: p. 65; Leo de Wys Inc./Leonard Harris: p. 35; Leo de Wys Inc./ Steve Vidler: p.83; Leo de Wys Inc./Wolfgang Hille: pp. viii, 63; *Milwaukee Journal*: p. 45; NASA: pp. 7, 29; *The New York Times*: pp. 51, 102; Photo Edit/David Young-Wolff: p. 73; Photo Researchers, Inc. Rafael Macia: p. 17; Photo Researchers, Inc./Richard Hutchings: p. 40; R. Hagan/Picture Group 1988: p. 43; Reynolds Metals Company, Richmond, Virginia: p. 89; Robert Marston and Associates, Inc.: p. 67; Superstock, Inc.: pp. 21, 32, 33, 69; United Press International Photo, Inc.: pp. 36, 46; Pat Brigandi: p. 103.

Cover photo:

Photo Researchers, Inc./Rafael Macia.

ISBN 0-590-46024-2

12 11 10 9 8 7 6 5 4 3 2 1   3 4 5 6 7 8/9

Printed in the U.S.A.   28

First Scholastic printing, April 1993

Contents

GARBAGE!

The Trashiest Book You'll Ever Read

Garbage, garbage everywhere!

1
Garbage:
The Never-ending Story

What Do We Mean by Garbage?

Funk & Wagnall's Standard Dictionary defines garbage as "1. Refuse from a kitchen, etc., consisting of unwanted or unusable pieces of meat, vegetable matter, eggshells, etc. 2. Anything worthless or offensive."

But garbage has come a long way from this definition. Garbage is solid waste, whether it's organic, petroleum-based (such as plastics or oil), radioactive, chemical, or even revolving around the earth like tiny moons!

How Long Has Garbage Been Around?

The first litterbugs were probably Adam and Eve. According to the Bible, they were thrown out of the Garden of Eden because they ate an apple that they weren't supposed to touch. Unless they

1

ate the entire apple, some of it ended up as Garden of Eden garbage. From that day on, humans have been tossing their leftover waste and hoping it will go away.

Scientists have wondered about humanity's deep-seated belief that garbage will not follow us. Some think our earliest ancestors lived in trees. Anything they tossed hit the ground and was never seen again. We still feel that this is the way it should be. Others feel that, as the only animal that walked upright, we were less likely to run into our leavings nose-first. Fido buried his bones — we walked over ours.

A Short History of Garbage

We'll never know exactly where our attitudes about garbage come from. But we do know how long the garbage dump has been around. When archaeologists want to know the real inside story of ancient humans, they find our ancestors' garbage piles, or "middens." That's where prehistoric people threw their leftovers from meals, old flint tools, and anything else they didn't want.

When people began to settle down and live in towns, the garbage settled down, too. Much of it was dumped inside onto the floor, or outside onto the street.

According to archaeologists, the ancient city of Troy rose to new heights on its old garbage. When the Trojans couldn't stand inside litter any longer, they didn't sweep up. They covered the garbage over with a new coating of clay flooring. Bingo — no more garbage! But over time, their living places got higher and higher.

In 1973 Charles Gunnerson, a civil engineer, measured Troy's uplift and figured that its citizens had covered over about 4.7 feet of garbage per century.

Troy isn't the only place to rise above itself. Roman ruins are several feet below modern Rome. And remains of New Amsterdam (the original Dutch name for Manhattan) are now anywhere from six to fourteen feet below modern Manhattan!

A lot of ancient garbage was burned. But a lot more was thrown into the streets. Human and animal scavengers got rid of the edibles, wearables, or usables outside.

In some ancient societies, the right to use or sell anything a person found was a scavenger's "pay." In return, these people became the first sanitation workers. They took *all* the street debris out of town into early versions of the town dump.

What Kinds of Garbage Are There?

Natural Garbage. Mother Nature is responsible for some garbage. Jillions of leaves fall off quadrillions of trees every year. Animals urinate, defecate, and shed hair wherever they live.

Trees, other plants, and animals will eventually die, leaving their remains. Natural mass kill-offs such as disease or starvation may kill an entire group of animals. Salmon die after spawning. And let's not forget nature's biggest kill-off — dinosaurs!

Personal Garbage. Organic personal garbage is what people usually think of when the word *garbage* comes up. It can be leftovers from a meal, chicken bones, potato peels, onion skins, cigarette butts, or the moldy carrots that were so cheap last spring.

Organic garbage includes things we don't like to think about, like bathroom flushings, disposable diaper waste, and pet litter from the family cat, dog, bird, or hamster.

Inorganic personal waste can be metal, glass, or plastic (such as trash bags!). Some inorganic personal waste is hazardous. This includes drain cleaners, bleach, window cleaners, tile and tub cleaners, oven cleaners, wood stains, varnishes, car fuel additives, old motor oil, degreasers, weed killers and other lawn care products, leftover medicines, the acid in batteries, and paint or paint thinners. Even nail polish, hair dyes, perfumes, and hair gels contain chemicals dangerous if they get into soil or water.

Industrial Garbage. Whenever industry makes a product, something is left over. Known as "by-products," most end up as sludge. Some industrial by-products are reusable. Animal bones can be

*Garbage comes in many forms. Here, a factory
dumps chemical waste into a nearby river.*

ground and used as fertilizer. Others, such as chemicals used to make products, may not be reusable. They might be burned. But even then, the ash left must be disposed of safely.

Hazardous Garbage. Leftover or discontinued chemicals must be disposed of, or stored where they will be harmless to humans. Medical waste can be hazardous waste. After all, one reason why people are in hospitals is so that their diseases will not be caught by healthy people. Their personal garbage, and even wastes such as blood and vomit, could be hazardous.

The nuclear age has brought a new, very dangerous garbage to the world — radioactive waste. This type of waste is left over from nuclear energy plants, medical facilities, military use, and even objects shot into space. Exposure to radioactive garbage is very dangerous, and this type of waste does not become harmless for thousands of years.

Plastics are another substance that came along with the twentieth century. There are hundreds of different types. Plastic is a good-news-bad-news substance. It's cheap, unbreakable, and can be made into all sorts of useful things. But plastics don't rot, which makes them very bad for landfills, litter, and water dumping. Many plastics can't be burned, either, because they give off toxic fumes.

Space Garbage. Does this sound far out? It is! Space is now littered with thousands of bits of things we humans have shot into the air.

"Space junk" used to be a curiosity. Now it is a danger. Since Russia's first satellite, *Sputnik*, went up in 1957, almost twenty thousand objects have been launched into space. Many of them fall out of orbit and burn up as they hit Earth's atmosphere. But thousands of objects will continue to revolve around us forever.

This computer-generated image shows the location of satellites and space debris in low Earth orbit.

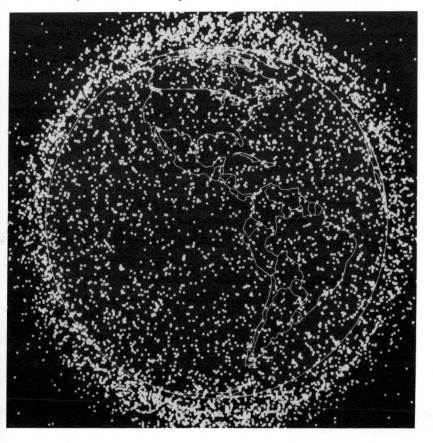

2
Good-bye Forever, or Is It?

Most modern methods of garbage disposal boil down to the same ideas that ancient humans had: 1) put it far enough away so that you don't see or smell it, 2) burn it, 3) find another use for it, 4) make less garbage to throw out.

Method one is by far the most popular. We carefully gather up various kinds of solid waste and dump it somewhere.

Dumping Garbage on Land: Landfills

Most U.S. towns still use landfills as the final resting place for over seventy percent of their municipal solid waste. Garbage is picked up from household garbage cans, put into a big garbage truck, and taken away. The truck takes its contents to a landfill. Pickup firms pay a "tipping fee" to dump the load into a landfill. Once in a landfill,

*Burning trash is one method of "getting rid"
of garbage. Can you think of any others?*

the garbage will supposedly rot, making room for more garbage.

Landfills used to be known as the town dump. They were open, smelly pits. Nobody uses the "D" word anymore. And modern landfill operators must meet a variety of health restrictions. To make sure that harmful materials don't get into surrounding soil and water, a landfill can't be placed near an airport runway, in wetlands or areas with a high floodplain, near a geologic fault line, or in an earthquake area.

New landfills must be lined with both compacted soil or clay, and a "membrane" liner to keep garbage leakings out of the surrounding soil. Plus there must be a collection system at the bottom to keep those leakings to about twelve inches or so.

Operators must cover each day's worth of garbage with a layer of soil, test samples for disease control, deal with potentially explosive gases (especially methane), have controls for storm water, and keep accurate records of how much garbage has gone where.

Does this sound like a lot of work for garbage? It is! And it's expensive. Construction of a well-run landfill can be as high as $750,000 per acre. But a well-maintained landfill can make as much as $250,000 per acre-*foot*, giving garbage a place to go.

In the United States alone, 180 million tons of solid waste are thrown out every year. If all that garbage were put into trucks, the line would reach halfway to the moon! By the year 2000, the United States could be tossing well over 190 million tons of garbage per year.

Why isn't this good news for landfills? Because half of the 5,500 landfills in the United States today will be full by the mid-1990s. New landfill sites aren't being opened as fast as old ones are closing down. More garbage plus less space equals today's garbage crunch!

Hey, what about the original landfill plan — the one that says garbage rots and makes room for other garbage? Surprise! Landfill garbage is so tightly compacted that very little air, light, and moisture gets in. Without air and moisture, trash actually preserves itself. Our garbage is mummified.

Archaeologist William L. Rathje has been studying landfills and garbage-in-the-can since 1973 as part of his University of Arizona Garbage Project.

The Garbage Project. Other archaeologists look into ancient midden heaps. Rathje digs into modern-day middens to find out about modern lives from the 1940s to yesterday. The Garbage Project folks can tell what kinds of garbage were thrown away in which decades. Their studies answer questions such as: Do consumers use more plastic now than ten or twenty years ago? How much more?

Garbage Project workers have hands-on (yech!) experience digging into landfills in Chicago, San Francisco, Tucson, Phoenix, and New York City. They wear protective clothing and face masks. The

11

Garbage Project has weighed and sorted over sixteen thousand pounds of garbage. What they found surprised everyone.

It turns out that fast-food packaging and disposable diapers made much less actual garbage than people had supposed. "The real culprit in every landfill," Rathje reported, "is plain old paper." The Garbage Project found that telephone books, newspapers, and construction debris such as bricks, concrete, and wood from torn-down buildings are the lion's share of each landfill.

Discarded tires are also a big problem. Most garbage gets crushed down from the weight of more garbage on top of it. Tires don't squish. They pop up to the top of the pile, no matter how much garbage is on top of them. Tires don't rot and when they catch on fire, it's hard to put out. Rats and insects hide and breed on the insides of old tires. Old tires, it seems, never die.

Landfills: The Trashiest Place in the World

Fresh Kills Landfill, on Staten Island, New York, is the largest landfill in existence. It opened in 1948, and it's just about full. This landfill takes up over three thousand acres and accepts seventeen thousand tons of refuse from New York City a day, six days a week. According to statistics, Fresh Kills Landfill may become the world's largest man-made object by the end of 1992. It will beat out the Great Wall of China.

Landfills: The Barge to Nowhere

New York's garbage problem, and the problem of landfills in general, were highlighted in 1988, with the famous "barge to nowhere." The garbage scow *Mobro 4000* was originally hired to take 3,186 tons of debris to a landfill in Islip, New York. No way, said the Islip dump — we don't have room.

What to do? The barge, hauled by the tugboat *Break of Dawn*, tried to find another place for its ripening cargo. It tried North Carolina, Florida, Alabama, Mississippi, and Louisiana — each time

If we don't take garbage seriously, scenes like this New York City skyline might become more common.

it was turned away. Then it tried Mexico, Belize, and the Bahamas. No deal.

By now newspapers had headlines like, "How Now, Foul Scow." The *Mobro 4000* was a worldwide laughingstock. Finally, the six-month-old trash was burned. It became trash ash — and ended up in the original Islip, New York landfill!

Landfills: NIMBY

Everybody wants garbage taken away. But nobody wants it near them. NIMBY stands for "Not In My Back Yard." Homeowners worry that having a landfill nearby will draw rats and roaches, smell bad, and cause the value of their property to go down.

Three real estate professors decided to put this theory to the test. For ten years they kept track of houses in two areas — one not near a landfill, and the other near a well-managed San Fernando Valley landfill.

All the homes studied were matched up as to how old the houses were, how big or small they were, and the ethnic makeup, family size, and income of each household. Also, the landfill had to be safe, not visible to the surrounding neighborhood, and patrolled to keep litter from flying out of the dump and onto neighboring property.

Records of house sales in both areas were carefully kept from 1978–1988. The resulting data showed that having a well-managed, well-designed landfill near a neighborhood does not bring property values down.

Landfills: Take Our Garbage — Please!

Traditionally, landfills are as far away from human habitats as possible. And the big waste companies are looking for isolated areas in which to build mega-dumps.

One company has its eye on a two-mile long, half-mile wide, quarter-mile deep former iron ore mine. The hole is already there, they argue. A system of liners would protect surrounding soil and water, they say. And it could hold one hundred years of trash at twenty thousand tons a day.

Two other companies are eyeing desert areas for mega-dumps. One wants to haul garbage deep into the desert on a Trash Train! Environmentalists worry that mega-dumps might hurt the delicate balance of nature in the desert. On the other hand, there's a lot of money involved. The county where the abandoned iron ore mine is could take in as much as $30 million a year in "host fees." And there would be jobs in hauling the garbage and managing the dumps.

West Virginia faced a mega-dump decision in 1991. Its dump would fill a six-thousand-acre hollow in a remote area of the state. The only town nearby was three miles away. The nontoxic waste would come in a Trash Train — 150 to 200 carloads per day.

In return, the landfill developers promised jobs, tax revenues, and a cleanup of the local river, which is where the local town's raw sewage had been going. The town, mostly made up of out-of-work miners, has been deeply divided about making a living off other people's garbage. Sure they need the money, but at what price? "In my heart I'm mad about it," says the town's newspaper publisher, "but I don't see anything else."

Old Landfills Never Fade Away

In the bad old days a filled landfill was covered over and forgotten about. Sometimes new buildings were built over the old site.

Residents of a Georgia subdivision built in 1985 didn't know their houses were sitting on top of a defunct garbage heap. One day a resident noticed that his windows wouldn't close. Then his doors wouldn't shut. That week, a three-inch opening developed in his floor. What was happening?

Officials checked records and realized that the old landfill underneath the new subdivision was filling up with methane gas. Methane will burn and, if contained in, say, a house where the gas is coming through the floor, it will explode.

Faced with the prospect of exploding houses, county officials closed the division and told everyone to evacuate. The area contained forty-four homes. The families that lived there had their lives suddenly uprooted and made into a nightmare, all because of garbage.

Landfills and Wildlife

One person's garbage is another's dinner. For better or worse, wildlife has found that dumps — especially open pits — are good sources of year-round goodies.

Joanna Burger and Michael Gochfeld watched birds at the Fresh Kills Landfill and found that their entire life-style revolves around the dumping schedule. Different species of birds have established a "pecking order" of who gets first pick, and who scavenges where.

Some birds actually follow the dump's bulldozers as they scoop over the top layer, exposing scraps underneath. They know when the operators start work, and the birds show up as if punching a time card.

Gulls hover and dip down for garbage the way they would dip into the ocean for fish. They also know how to rip into plastic to get at the goods. Younger birds learn from the older ones. Bigger birds steal from smaller ones.

A city dump becomes a banquet for hungry sea gulls.

Another study found that the brown snake is a happy wildlife camper in landfills. Because of the heat generated by decomposition, snakes can regulate their temperature year-round. There are lots of mice, rats, and insects to eat. Garbage provides plenty of handy hiding places.

In places near wilderness areas, dumps bring close encounters on the wild side. Bears are especially likely to forage in a dump area. Sometimes they don't stop there, and end up in town or running into campers. Small towns in Alaska put up with periodic polar bear invasions, especially when food in the wild becomes scarce. Sometimes, when a bear becomes a threat to the population, it must be destroyed.

Even game reserve animals are not immune to dump feeding. Tourists in Kenya, Africa, come to look at wildlife in the native savannah. But if they want to see baboons, hyenas, and vultures, they'd have more luck at the hotel dump, where the animals go to chow down on scraps.

Landfills: How Much Is Cleanliness Worth?

Managing garbage in landfills is a serious and expensive business. Tax dollars paid for old dumps are small potatoes compared to what's needed for state-of-the-art landfill costs.

People wouldn't really rather wallow in garbage than pay for its disposal! But as one environmental executive said, "Eventually, people are going to ask, 'How clean is clean?' It's a question for which we have no answer."

Littering

Nobody likes litter. But litter didn't arrive all by itself. In this case we have seen the enemy — and it is US!

For many years, Americans didn't think much about tossing wrappers, cans, or leftovers out of car windows or underfoot. When litter became a nationwide disgrace, the organization *Keep America Beautiful* helped Americans become aware of the problem. With KAB's help, citizens began to organize and clean up their (our) act!

But the problem of litter is certainly not over. A great deal of time and money is still spent picking up what we toss from cars, or simply drop on the ground without thinking. Where did your last gum wrapper go?

Litter sometimes kills. Lighted cigarettes tossed from cars can set fire to dry brush and start forest fires. A lot of wildlife die in those fires. When fires get out of control, they threaten nearby houses.

Litter is not something that giant corporations or governments force on helpless citizens. Litter is personal. It is the one form of garbage that we as individuals have total, complete control over. It can stop today, if we just don't do it.

3
Dumping, Dumping, Everywhere

Dumping Garbage in Water

What do you think about when you pour something down a drain or flush a toilet? If you're like most people, you figure the bad stuff is gone and the world's a cleaner place.

But all waste must go somewhere. This stuff ends up in a wastewater treatment plant. There, sewage and other water wastes are broken down into sludge. Thanks to the Water Pollution Control Act of 1972, untreated sludge or industrial waste doesn't find its way directly into rivers and lakes anymore. Also, because of new pollution regulations, many outdated wastewater treatment plants must be rebuilt or updated.

Urban treatment plants tend to get more money and faster help, because contaminated city water could cause a huge epidemic. But over half of all

Would you want to swim here?
Wastewater treatment plants clean up a lot of
water pollution, but there's still more to do.

small-town water treatment plants need updating within the next ten years — a $2.4 billion project. It will take a lot of money and work to get the country's water treatment plants able to deal with the amount and types of waste going (literally) down the drain.

Dumping Garbage in Davy Jones's Locker

What convenient dump is big, out of sight and smell, and not in anyone's backyard? The ocean!

Plenty of garbage hits the drink. Debris from the fishing industry and offshore oil operations is thrown into the ocean without a second thought. Every merchant ship packs a two- to three-month supply of whatever the crew of twenty-five or so people per ship need. Their garbage walks the plank. Even the U.S. Navy dumps about four tons of plastics alone into the oceans every day.

Plastic is an especially bad thing to leave in an ocean. It doesn't rot. Wildlife doesn't know to stay away from it. Seals get tangled in lost plastic fishing nets. Unable to swim up for air, they drown. Diving birds pick up lost or cast-off fishing lines. They can't get the stuff off. It wraps around them like a snake and can eventually tangle up their legs, wrap around a wing, or get them caught in a tree later where they hang and starve. Starved pelicans have been found with their beaks closed by a beverage container ring. When curious seals poke their noses through plastic six-pack rings, they can't get them off, and drown. Leatherback turtles mistake floating plastic bags for their normal diet of jellyfish. The plastic goes in, but it doesn't come out. Too many of these mistakes might be a turtle's last.

Boaters' engines are damaged when a plastic bag wraps around their propellers. Human divers have gotten tangled in old fishing lines and bits of net.

Another form of ocean dumping is beach litter. It ruins valuable property, and can make a day on the beach a nightmare if you step on a broken bottle or a hypodermic needle half-buried in sand.

During the summers of 1987 and 1988 ocean dumping of medical waste made a big splash on

This man has to be extremely careful! He's collecting dangerous medical debris that washed up at high tide.

East coast beaches. A waste company illegally dumped hazardous medical waste into the Atlantic Ocean. Unfortunately, it washed back onto public beaches. Suddenly, sunbathers were stepping over blood vials and surgical gloves. They were also in danger of stepping on hypodermic needles — some of them still infected with hepatitis or the AIDS virus.

The very worst ocean dumping is usually not intentional. Oil spills are an ecological nightmare that is not going to go away.

Fully loaded with Alaskan oil intended for Exxon, the tanker *Valdez* hit an underwater reef on March 24, 1989. Eleven million gallons of oil spilled into Alaska's once-beautiful Prince William Sound.

The *Valdez* had the latest safety equipment, the weather was good, and the ship's radio was in range of both coastal radar and Coast Guard operators. How could this have happened?

Everyone was caught off guard. The first company to the rescue had some of its equipment on the blink, and a lot of their crew was gone because the accident happened on Good Friday — just before the Easter weekend. By the time Exxon got in over the weekend, the oil slick had spread over nine hundred square miles of water. All the pumping, dispersing agents, containment plans, and oil-burning equipment couldn't stop the slime.

Once valuable oil, the spillage was now garbage. Miles of coastline were covered in tarlike goo. Some coasts had a six-inch coat of the stuff.

Oil that sank to the bottom of the sound will stay there for years. Only time will tell the effect of weathered oil on clams, mussels, crabs, plankton, barnacles, snails, and fish eggs. As the oil that hit the shores hardens, it becomes a layer of asphalt just under the shore surface. It is supposed to be harmless. But can wild animals that build tunnels and burrows dig through asphalt?

The *Valdez* cleanup was incredibly expensive. Everything and everybody had to be flown or shipped into this remote area. In order for the cleanup crews to operate, they needed 9.8 million pounds of groceries, 530 miles of toilet paper,

A containment boom extends around the Exxon Valdez in a desperate effort to prevent gallons of oil from seeping into the Prince William Sound.

This bird is one of the unfortunate victims of the Valdez *oil spill.*

564,000 pairs of rubber gloves, 125,000 coveralls, 157,000 sets of rain gear, 65,000 pairs of boots, 225 inflatable boats, 700 outboards, 275 skiffs, 350 electricity generators, 875 pumps, and 174 cars and trucks!

During the Persian Gulf War, an oil spill in that gulf was a deliberate act of war by Iraq. As the Iraqis retreated from Kuwait at the end of that war, they also set fire to Kuwait's many desert oil wells. It added incredible air pollution to incredible water pollution. Together, these acts added up to the worst spill in history.

As oil poured out of uncapped wells, tens of

A Kuwaiti oilfield worker kneels for midday prayers near one of the many burning oil fields in his country.

millions of barrels' worth became "oil lakes" on what had been desert sands. Desert plants and animals were engulfed. Birds fooled into thinking the liquid was a real lake made their final mistake landing on it.

Oil in the Persian Gulf smeared beaches and sank to the bottom, smothering sea life in an oily brown blanket. A year later, in 1991, water around Abu Ali Island was still the color of bouillon.

Smoke from well fires rose into a plume stretching over sixty miles. Ground pollution from airborne particles didn't reach normal levels for one hundred miles. Planes flying through the mess came out streaked with oil.

Space — Garbage's Final Dumping Frontier

You look into the sky one night and make a wish on a shooting star. Darn! It wasn't a shooting star at all — just another chunk of space junk reentering the atmosphere!

Space junk is classified by size into particles, fragments, and artifacts. *Particles* are under four inches in diameter, like exhaust particles and paint chips. *Fragments* can be up to 3.28 feet and include bolts loosened during launch. *Artifacts* are larger — like entire rocket stages dropped off on the way up!

You may think that the bigger the object, the more dangerous it is. Not necessarily! In 1983 a paint chip traveling at eight thousand miles an hour hit a window on the *Challenger* while it was

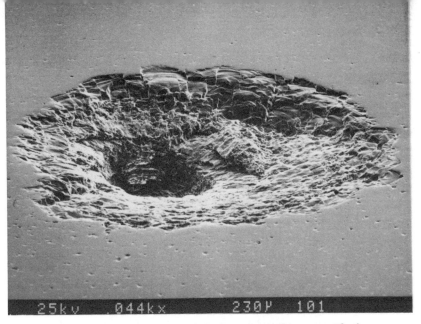

*Can you guess what this is? Greatly magnified,
it is a picture of the damage a paint chip did
to the window of the Space Shuttle* Challenger.

in orbit. The pea-sized hole it made cost about
$50,000 to repair. It makes one wonder what the
electric screwdriver that floated away from an as-
tronaut in 1984 could do!

In 1986 the European *Ariane* booster rocket ex-
ploded from its own unused fuel and sent booster
fragments all over the place. That was accidental.
But other objects have been intentionally blown
up. According to the National Security Council, in
1989, "The major contributor to the increase in
orbital debris in recent years has been the
U.S.S.R.'s deliberate destruction of military satellites which have malfunctioned."

Space junk is a problem that won't go away. Because space has no atmosphere, it doesn't rot. And because there's no friction, it doesn't slow down either. At the time of this writing, there is no real policy about reducing what's going up, or cleaning up what's there.

So what's being done? Scientists are looking into fuels that will not leave particles in space, paints that won't flake off as much, and rocket stages that won't be orbiting with explosive fuel left in them. They're also planning a space garbage truck called an OMV (orbital maneuvering vehicle). The OMV would orbit high in space, picking up large pieces of space junk, and moving them down far enough so that they would enter the Earth's atmosphere and burn up.

A space "net" is also under discussion, but there are bugs that need to be worked out. At the moment a net can't tell what's garbage — and what's a working satellite.

4
Other Options

Burning Garbage: Up in Smoke

One age-old method of getting rid of garbage is to burn it. Since most garbage is paper, it is easy enough to burn and it creates energy. This burning of trash can be translated into electricity.

Waste-to-energy plants became big business in the early 1970s. By the mid-1990s, these plants will be supplying five to twenty percent of U.S. electricity.

Some of the waste burned gives off poisonous fumes. Waste-to-energy incinerators must be fitted with air pollution devices to keep harmful emissions out of the air. Ashes left from burning some wastes may also be hazardous. Plants must dispose of both hazardous and nonhazardous ashes.

Many incinerators are not geared for getting en-

Burning garbage can be a way of creating energy,
but it can also be harmful to the environment.

ergy from trash burning. They just get rid of trash.
Many municipal incinerators are old. They weren't
built to handle the burning of substances like
plastic, which can send toxins into the air. Their
smokestacks supposedly rise high enough to keep
anything noxious away from the humans below.
But city dwellers where older incinerators still
work can tell by the occasional rains of ash that
this isn't true.

Anyone who has a fireplace knows what a pain
leftover ashes can be. When you burn a hundred
tons of garbage, you're left with thirty tons of ash!
Cadmium and lead in ashes from burning batteries and plastics make some ash hazardous.

Where are incinerator ashes taken? Municipal

Medical waste must be treated with extreme caution.

ash is usually taken to already overcrowded landfills.

Two thirds of all medical waste is burned. Medical waste can be blood, nose secretions, body fluids, bile, any human tissue, or even medical cultures and anything in contact with sick people, such as surgical gloves, sheets, or bandages. Hospitals, doctors' and dentists' offices, mortuaries, blood banks, research laboratories, outpatient clinics, nursing homes, veterinary clinics, and in-home care all have medical waste.

Burning infected items and many plastics makes it very important to have up-to-date incinerator systems for this kind of trash. Unfortunately, most hospital incinerators are not up-to-date.

Use It Again, Sam — Recycling

Recycling is not new. Once, ragpickers paid a small sum for discarded cloth, which they later sold to paper mills. Scrap metal dealers crushed old cars, broken appliances, and other metal goods and sold the scrap to metal industries. Poor folks went to junkyard owners to buy spare car parts, used-but-still-working appliances, sinks, or lawn-mowers that had seen better days.

Now junkyards are out. Waste management systems are in. But the idea of making something used into something usable is the same.

Though recycling isn't new, the things we recycle and the huge amounts involved are different. Many communities recycle voluntarily. In other places, it is mandatory. Businesses required to recycle their materials can be fined if they don't.

Recycling has some problems. People will recycle as long as it's no trouble. Curbside pickup is a landslide favorite over taking recyclables to a drop-off site. Separating recyclables is another problem. You separate the paper, plastic, and glass at home. But someone has to get the green and amber glass away from the clear glass. Different types of plastics and of paper must be separated. And cans of different metals must be separated. Finally, recycling plants must be able to make the materials into something useful.

Plants must be able to handle what they get. A Tucson, Arizona, center was swamped by public response to a 1991 glass collecting campaign. As a result, a lot of that glass ended up in a landfill!

*Scrap metal dealers used to sell their
"junk" to metal industries.*

In the 1970s and 1980s people laughed at recycling. At first, recycled goods cost more than "new" ones! But as the initial cost of building recycling plants has been met, recycling is making a lot of dollars and sense.

Aluminum cans are a case in point. Recycling cans means a can company doesn't have to find, mine, and refine aluminum ore. "Ninety-five percent of the energy is saved when you recycle a can," said an Alcoa regional director.

Making Less of a Bad Thing

Rather than trying to find more places to dump more garbage, how about making less garbage to dump?

This "mountain" of recyclable aluminum cans was collected in one week. It's estimated that over two billion cans are recycled every year!

Overpackaged goods are a problem. Foods are "double-wrapped." We make some homemade popcorn on the stove and then toss the aluminum pan, its wire handle, the cardboard label, and the folded aluminum that puffed up when the corn popped. Inks for the computer used to write this book came in a cardboard box. Inside that was a tin pan with an aluminum peel-off top. *That* held a plastic pan with the actual plastic ink holder in it. And when the ink runs out — the ink holder will be thrown out as well!

What is the solution? A tax on packaging? Legislation? Packaging made from recycled goods? Only time will tell!

The Twentieth Century, and Welcome to It: What to Do with Nuclear Waste?

Before World War II, there was no nuclear waste. Now there's plenty, left over from military and peaceful use of nuclear facilities.

Between the years 1946 and 1982, a lot of nuclear waste was quietly put in metal drums lined with concrete and dropped into the ocean. The Atlantic and Pacific oceans got most of the waste, dumped mainly by Great Britain and the United States. Other contributors were Switzerland, the Netherlands, France, Belgium, West Germany, Italy, Sweden, Japan, and New Zealand. To this day, nobody knows exactly how much radioactive material ended up in the ocean, or exactly where it is.

The trouble with radioactive waste is not only

that it's dangerous, but that it's dangerous for so *long*! It takes 10,000 years to convert into a less dangerous form and it's not completely safe for 240,000 years!

As of 1990, ninety-five million gallons of high-level military nuclear waste is being held at temporary sites while a suitable permanent site solution is being found. Meanwhile, some of this waste is in danger of leaking through forty-five-year-old corroding metal containers.

The U.S. government hopes to permanently bury the waste under Yucca Mountain, in Nevada. The mountain is ninety miles northwest of Las Vegas. Its nearest neighbor is a nuclear test site, so there are already tight restrictions about anyone being on-site. Its remoteness and dryness make possible contamination of soil or water unlikely.

Whatever scientists decide, they'd better be right. As the magazine *US News and World Report* put it, "By the year 2000, the nation will have produced 48,000 tons of high-level nuclear waste. . . . Every speck of this refuse is intensely poisonous."

In New Mexico, Nevada's neighbor, an ex-salt mine may be a permanent resting place for low-level military radioactive waste. Compared to Yucca Mountain's waste, radioactive levels of this solid waste is not high. But this stuff isn't going to be completely safe for 240,000 years!

Here's the plan. Salt beds will be hollowed out into a honeycomb of chambers. One chamber will be filled with barrels for five years, and then watched. If all goes well, more barrels will go into the chambers — up to a million barrels in twenty-five years.

When the chambers are filled, they will be sealed. The ground above will be decontaminated. And the site will be abandoned. Supposedly within a hundred years or so, salt will grow around the barrels, sealing them forever. But how are a million barrels of waste going to be safely transported to the salt mine? What if a truck overturns or a railroad accident happens? Worse, what if cavern moisture and salt form a corrosive that, instead of sealing everything in, eats through the barrels and sucks the bad stuff out?

As New Mexico State Senator Tom Rutherford said, "We have waste we aren't sure about, in containers that haven't been approved, traveling over roads that haven't been improved, being put in salt beds that we don't know about."

Dealing with Plastic

Plastic is another material that was not around before World War II. This new, cheap, pliable, and very useful material has become a garbage nightmare. Though it's not as dangerous as nuclear waste by a longshot, it stays around just about as long. The stuff doesn't seem to rot. And when burned, many plastics give off poisonous fumes. Plastic simply hasn't been around long enough for us to know what happens to it over time. What to do?

For many fast food restaurants, these nonrecyclable containers are a thing of the past.

Polystyrene is one type of plastic that's been getting a lot of attention lately. When fast food joints switched from wrapping food in paper bags to putting it in polystyrene containers, people were happy. Food didn't get squashed in the car, and it stayed warm longer. Styrofoam coffee cups didn't burn people's hands.

But by the early 1990s, consumers realized that the "clamshells" holding their burger might be around in a landfill for four hundred years!

Over eight hundred chapters of "Kids Against Pollution" organized against the use of polystyrene plastics.

Some fast food places listened. Some use paper wrapping again. Others recycle their polystyrene. It is broken down into "pebbles" first, and then used to make other plastic products — like, say, trash cans!

5
Making a Sad Song Better, First Verse

At the moment, eighty percent of solid waste from municipal areas is sent to landfills. Ten percent is burned. Ten percent is recycled. The U.S. Environmental Protection Agency's 1995 goal is twenty-percent incineration, twenty-five percent recycling, and fifty-five percent landfill.

This chapter and the next show ideas for making current disposal methods safer, and for finding better solutions for the future.

Better Landfills

Two solid waste landfills in Florida are helping landfill garbage to do what it's supposed to do — rot. Air and water are sent through the landfill in a maze of pipes to help the waste degrade more quickly. "We are trying to change the image of a landfill from a tomb to a reactor," said R. Jerry Murphy, head of the project. This method can completely break down landfill waste within five years. After that, the material left can be mined and sold as landfill cover dirt. The hole left will take on new garbage and the entire process will begin again.

Methane gas given off by landfills is the prime reason why dumps smell so bad. But methane is a usable fuel. New systems recover methane and carbon dioxide from landfills and use those gases to power electrical plants.

Utilities like the idea because landfill gas is cheaper than oil and doesn't leave ashes. Landfill operators like the idea of not having to burn off the gas themselves, and of making a buck, even from a full landfill!

What do you do with an old, full landfill? Newark and JFK International airports are built on former landfills. Others become golf courses or parks. But building anything over an old landfill needs careful planning.

Cambridge, Massachusetts city officials took ten years to study their situation before they built a new park over an old landfill. What had gone into the landfill? Toxins? Radioactive material? Anything dangerous that could leak into the surrounding soil or water? Would the area seep methane gas? Would trash settle, causing sudden holes?

Developers not only did their own studies — they took questions and suggestions from official

What would you do with an old, full, landfill?

groups, environmental groups, neighborhood associations, and private citizens. The end result is a park that was well-planned, meets the local needs, and is a place where people feel safe.

Water, Water

Arizona, arid to begin with, can't afford to contaminate its water. So everyone was alarmed to learn that chemicals from a nearby air force plant were leaching into underground aquifers where Tucson's drinking water was coming from.

Air Force and community banded together in 1987 to open a new water treatment plant. The plant not only takes care of daily contamination, but is correcting past contamination. Aquifer water is pumped out, run through several stages of filters and treatment vessels until it is quality drinking water again, and pumped back into the aquifer.

Lowelville, Ohio (pop. 1,349), made a deal between their landfill and sewage treatment plants to help one another.

The landfill operator helped update the treatment plant. In return, the treatment plant will siphon off and treat the landfill's "leachate."

Leachate is the slimy stuff at the bottom of a landfill where liquids collect. These liquids can be anything from newsprint ink to hair dye, and it's a witch's brew of noxious substances.

The landfill operator benefits from having his leachate made squeaky clean. The water treatment plant benefits from being built to state-of-the-art form, practically free of charge. The community benefits with clean soil and water handled by up-to-date facilities.

Cocoa, Florida, expects its population to boom to twice its current size within fifteen years. Besides expanding its wastewater treatment plant, it needed a better way of cleaning up sludge before discharging it into the local ecosystem — in this case, a lagoon.

Wastewater treatment operators found a bacteria that loves to chow down on waste material. Then "We tricked them," said the plant Utility Di-

Wastewater treatment plants are instrumental in preserving our ecosystem.

rector, "into eating what they normally wouldn't."

After the stressed-out, hungry bacteria did their work, Cocoa had water clean enough to use for watering parks, lawns, and highway medians. Their drinking water was left for drinking.

Los Angeles used to discharge its sludge into the ocean, but no more. Now it takes twelve hundred wet tons of sludge per day, dries it into "sludge cake" and burns it for energy. Some of the resulting ash is used in a copper plant, and other uses for it are being investigated.

Sludge cakes not burned are chemically treated and used as landfill cover. Others are mixed with yard trimmings and composted.

The icing on the sludge cake is that Los Angeles' plan actually saves about $6 million a year over conventional plants of the same size.

Incineration

Hospitals are looking for ways to incinerate their hazardous waste safely. Some up-to-date incinerators spray a fine mist of lime and water into the incinerator flue whenever waste is burned. The combination forms a calcium salt that collects and absorbs toxic flue gases before they hit the atmosphere. Others use ever-smaller filters to keep ever-

*Improved systems of incineration
are being developed.*

smaller ashes from getting into the atmosphere. The ash is carefully removed, put inside a sealed bag, and taken to a landfill site that handles hazardous waste.

Winston-Salem, North Carolina, uses a system that came from West Germany. The bulk of their hazardous waste is shredded, sprayed with steam, and then disinfected by being zapped with microwaves! The resultant trash holds less bacteria than the average household's and can be taken to a local landfill. It can even be burned without danger of infectious or toxic gases hitting the atmosphere. The new system saved so much money that it paid for itself within three years.

Nuclear Storage

The problem of permanently storing nuclear waste is tremendous. A company named Concept RKK has come up with what it thinks is the perfect temporary solution. Its process, called Cryocell, would turn the ground around buried nuclear waste into permafrost. A fifty- to seventy-foot thick layer of solid frozen ground would keep every molecule inside, away from surrounding soil or water. Then, until a permanent site could be found, at least radioactive materials would be kept isolated.

Terran Environmental Inc. is testing another solution believed to be as good, and sixty percent cheaper, than any other temporary storage for nuclear and hazardous waste. Terran put calcium carbonate — a substance found in limestone — into the ground surrounding the toxic waste. In a few days, the substance bonds with surrounding rock and makes a kind of thick mud. In a few months, the calcium carbonate hardens into impenetrable rock itself. The toxic waste is sealed inside.

This sounds like a permanent solution but it's not. The calcium carbonate has to be kept to a certain alkaline level to stay in its rocklike form. Left to itself — well, who can tell what will happen in a hundred or a thousand years?

One interesting idea to come up for nuclear waste storage is, since the United States and the former Soviet Union have banned underground testing of nuclear weapons — how about using those former sites as dumps for nuclear waste? After all, if they were safe for testing, they *should* be safe for storing.

Plastics

Lately, there has been much talk about biodegradable plastics. The plan is to mix plastic with something like, say, cornstarch. When the plastic is thrown out, microbes eat the cornstarch, and the plastic is broken down into bits.

What's wrong with that? The microbes are still only eating the cornstarch — not the plastic. Now instead of a big plastic container left around for four hundred years, as an Environmental Defense Fund spokesperson said, " . . . what you leave behind is certainly less visible, but . . . more dangerous, plastic dust."

*Recycling plastics is one great
way kids can help out!*

Why more dangerous? A gallon milk jug won't leach into the water system, but plastic dust could. A bird or mammal isn't likely to eat that jug. But they might pick up post-cornstarch plastic bits! And mixing the plastic won't mean less plastic, either. Because the organic material weakens the plastic, the plastic used will have to be thicker than what's used now. If only researchers could figure a way to make cartons entirely out of cornstarch!

"Photodegradable" plastic, also known as sun sacks, is available now in some markets. Ultraviolet sunlight rays shred this type of plastic over a period of about six weeks. Eventually the plastic melts away completely.

This sounds perfect. But one problem here is space. Landfill isn't spread out so that every piece of garbage gets six weeks in the sun. Also, garbage bags made of photodegradable plastic will cost more than other kinds.

But wouldn't this solve litter problems? Maybe. Environmentalists worry that because people think that photodegradable plastics will "go away," they'll stop feeling guilty about tossing litter around. The result, they say, might be *more* litter!

Still, sun sacks offer some hope of dealing with plastic pollution. British Columbia has been using sun sacks since 1988. Hefty began to offer these bags in 1990. The label claims they are a "step in our commitment to a better environment." The world is anxiously waiting to see if that's so.

*Landfills take up so much space that it would be
easy to get lost in one. Look closely . . . how
many people can you find in this landfill?*

Toxic Avengers

In 350 B.C. the Chinese used tailor ants to keep
boring beetles from eating their fruit crops. A century ago, California's citrus industry was about to
be done in by a beetle that no chemicals at the
time could control. They imported Australian
ladybugs. When the Australian ladybug's less-
than-ladylike appetite bit the beetles, the beetles
bit the dust.

This method of fighting fire with fire, pestwise,
now has a name. It's called IPM, short for Integrated Pest Management. Farmers worldwide are
beginning to look at this old method of pest control
with new interest.

For a long time, the United States felt that finding the right poison for the right beast was the answer to pest control. Unfortunately, pests developed resistance to chemicals used. Instead of dead pests, we got super-pests. Plus, chemicals got into the soil, and sometimes into plants.

But, an advocate of IPM pointed out, even the most poison-resistant pest can't keep from being eaten. A hungry enemy doesn't care if that pest has an immunity to chemicals or not. It just chows down!

Nowadays, almond growers in California use predatory mites to take care of destructive red spiders. Indonesians supply farmers with bags of wolf spiders to control potentially disastrous brown planthoppers. Nigeria spreads a type of wasp over cassava fields like a crop duster. The wasps kill cassava mealybugs.

The Bio-Integral Resource Center in Berkeley, California, gathers as much information as possible about what eats what. That way if it is asked for suggestions, it can provide several species names that can get rid of what ails your crop.

Back to the Future

McDonald's was once nicknamed Ronald McToxic because of its use of polystyrene. Alarmed, many McDonald's are going back to paper packaging. As McDonald's President Edward Rensi said, ". . . our customers just don't feel good about [foam packaging]. So we're changing."

McDonald's is still not sure what to do about their plastic coffee cups, cutlery, or their overseas operations. But they are looking heavily into recycling.

Laws and local ordinances in some states are banning or limiting the use of polystyrene. New York has banned putting food that you're going to eat on the premises in a disposable wrap. Why wrap what you'll unwrap five seconds later? In addition, if you really must have a bag for your leftovers, it'll cost you a nickel.

"Greening" the Market

Marketing researchers agree that there is a demand for environmentally friendly products. But there is also a need for consumers to know which ones they are! Canadian and European stores have several methods of pointing these products out.

In America, San Diego's Big Bear Supermarkets put out cards and pamphlets listing products that the San Diego Environmental Health Coalition has dubbed environmentally friendly.

Wal-Mart is "greening" its own products, and letting consumers know about it. The improvement might be less packaging, a product that is more concentrated, or one that doesn't deplete Earth's ozone layer. Many stores also include recycling bins in their parking lots.

"The idea came mainly from our customers and

our employees," said Wal-Mart spokesperson Brenda Lockhart. " . . . they said the need for environmentally friendly products and packaging was a concern."

Less Packing, More Product

The United States is trying to reduce the amount of packaging that goods come in. One effort that is gaining in popularity is the idea of refills. Manufacturers used to sell consumers a plastic bottle of, say, fabric softener every time the consumer needed it. That meant every time the consumer ran out of the product, another plastic bottle hit the trash can and ultimately a landfill. Now, consumers buy one plastic bottle the first time, and the next time they get a refill of the product. The refill is packaged in a biodegradable box.

Proctor & Gamble, whose products are responsible for plenty of landfill, is trying new ideas within the company. They're testing Liquid Tide, Cheer, Downy, and Spic and Span in recycled plastic bottles. They're experimenting with products for which you buy a bottle the first time, and refills after that. They're mixing products such as detergent with bleach, and detergent with fabric softener, so that one package will be bought instead of two.

Some communities are trying a less-than-gentle nudge to get people to cut down their personal trash. Local laws require citizens to use city trash bags. You're charged for the bags. This way, the folks who throw away the most trash pay the most to have it taken away. If you don't use the city bags, the fine is $250. These communities have found their unrecycled curbside garbage went down by a third — right away!

*Hot off the presses! Paper dresses made
a fashion statement in the sixties.*

6
Recycling — Making a Sad Song Better, Second Verse

Paper

Paper is one of the fastest-growing recycled products. At first, consumers weren't sure about using used paper. Now they've seen it, and it doesn't look "used" or have accidental pieces of somebody's lunch pressed into it. Business brochures, newsletters, annual reports, and direct mail are routinely printed on recycled paper. And every ton of recycled paper used means seventeen trees are still in the ground!

Did you know that some of your newspaper may literally be old news? Many papers use recycled pulp mixed with new. So far, the *Los Angeles Times* uses the biggest mix — half their morning paper has been a paper before. Mixing old and new pulp is necessary. Recycled fibers break and become shorter every time they're used again. But don't worry. Newsprint can be recycled five to eight times before it has to become something else.

A 1960s fad for paper dresses quickly disintegrated — probably after the first rain. Now, Li Fu Chen of Purdue University has found a way of making rayon from low-grade cellulose such as recycled paper or even cornstalks!

There are no harmful by-products in the process. The resulting fiber is so chemical-free that it could be used for food packaging. The cloth is similar to raw silk and so strong that it can be made into tire cords — just like "real" rayon.

Li Fu Chen sees many uses for his new fiber. Besides cloth, it can be molded into a lightweight, strong substance for products like tennis rackets or automobile and airplane parts.

Compost

Gardeners have recycled leaves into compost for centuries. Now waste companies are composting both leaves and "leavings" — big time.

Waste companies shred organic waste, mechanically stir it every day, and blow air through it to help bacteria make waste into compost. Waste is temperature- and moisture-controlled to help the bacteria do their job well.

Oxygen-loving bacteria make the composting smell no worse than wet leaves. Keeping bacteria happy and hungry cuts composting time from up to a year to a matter of weeks.

Big-time composters aren't choosey. The array

of organic waste that can be composted is astounding. Sure, they use yard clippings and treated sewage sludge. They'll also use crab scraps, "trash" fish caught that nobody will eat, sawdust, entire failed crops, supermarket produce that didn't sell, and chicken parts not found in the grocery store! All this would have gone to landfill otherwise.

Upstate New York (Onondaga County) used a truly unusual compost mix — old NYNEX phone books and Anheuser-Busch brewery waste! In 1989 over 175 tons of old phone books were collected, shredded, and sent to the brewery. Brewers mixed their brewery waste with the phone books instead of the usual sawdust.

Anheuser-Busch got forty thousand cubic yards of nutrient-rich compost, sold to happy customers as rich garden soil. NYNEX got paid by the brewery for its telephone books instead of having to shell its own money out to a landfill company. And the county doesn't have a hundred thousand mummified phone books in its overcrowded landfill.

Composters have found that different microbes will eat different things. Some microbes chow down on toxic wastes. Others snack on oil. Some munch TNT. Bacteria that will eat uranium have even been found deep in the earth! This discovery has become "bio-remediation," a hot new science. Microbes may be our answer to cleaning up toxic soil or water, oil spills, and nuclear contamination.

Plastics

If plastic isn't going to rot away, we'd better find uses for it! A Florida firm, Mandish Research, is mixing polystyrene foam with concrete to make a lightweight building material called Donolite. Depending on what's being built, the Donolite may be anywhere from forty to eighty percent foam.

The company uses old coffee cups, clamshell containers, and used packing materials from high schools, vocational schools, and local retailers. Donolite is good for roofs and decks, where concrete would be too heavy, or it can be molded into outdoor ornaments such as birdbaths or porch pillars. It doesn't swell in the summer and shrink in the winter, so it doesn't crack over the years.

McDonald's has "McRecycle" projects. Besides recycling their remaining plastic goods, they also use recycled plastic (mainly computer housings) for roofing material. With three hundred new McDonald's built every year, and a thousand or so re-roofed every year, that's a LOT of roofing tile!

In 1990, McDonald's, Dow Chemical, Arco Chemical, Chevron Chemical, Mobil Chemical, and four other companies resolved to recycle polystyrene together as the National Polystyrene Recycling Company. By 1995 their goal is to recycle twenty-five percent of America's polystyrene.

They will take old polystyrene cups, plates, bowls, toys, etc., then grind, clean, and sell them. Companies like Rubbermaid can make new products from the recycled plastic. An office in-out box today may have been a coffee cup last year! Or your eggs may be in a carton that was last year's Big Mac carton!

Recycling plastics is catching on fast. At least seventy other firms are also looking into "plastics recovery and recycling."

One big headache is sorting the 2,700 types of plastic being turned out every day! You can't just melt all plastics down in the same vat because different plastics are made from different resins.

A possible answer is to make mixed plastic from recycled plastic! Polystyrene is being mixed with other plastics into "plastic lumber." This "wood-

What kinds of things will be made out of the plastics these kids are recycling? Park benches? Soda bottles? Paintbrushes?

less wood" can be used for public park benches and picnic tables, playground equipment, and highway posts.

Vinyl plastic is another good candidate for recycling. Plastic bottles made of vinyl are turned in. Then the plastic is reused in construction, such as vinyl siding, sewer pipes, or drain tiles. It could also be used to make garden hoses, flower vases, or office supplies — anything, in fact, that does not come into contact with food.

PET is short for polyethylene terephthalate. Your two-liter soda bottles are probably made out of it. They can be cleaned and crushed into pellets to be used in products like paint brushes, carpeting, boat sails, and fiberfill for ski jackets!

When autos were metal, they were crushed into unbelievably small box shapes and used for scrap metal. Now cars are made of more and more plastic. What happens when *these* cars are junked?

Auto makers hope that the very thing people fear — plastics that stay around forever — may make car #1 into car #2 and even car #3. Or, a car body's final resting place may be your home — GE has already made a model house using mainly recycled plastics. Instead of having a car in a garage, your old car may BE your new garage!

Used Tires

Oregon has an experiment using local scrap tires in road building. Here's how it works. When consumers buy new tires, they pay an extra dollar so

Cars made mainly out of metal used to end up in scrap yards like this.

they won't have to take the old tire home. That dollar pays to melt down the used tires and process them into an asphalt-rubber mix.

This mix's first "new" road is being studied for durability, cracking, potholes, and other possible problems. Oregon (and the rest of the country) has its fingers crossed!

Alaska, Arizona, and Washington grind old tires into "crumb rubber" and use it on their highways. They say these road surfaces are more resilient and that cars skid less in rainy, icy, or snowy conditions.

Always a problem, now landfill tires can be part of the solution. "Tire chips" are a new experiment in lining material for landfills.

Glass

Recycled glass bottles are sorted by color, cleaned, and crushed into a mush called "cullet." Second-time-around bottles are two thirds new materials, and one third cullet from recycled material. But some companies say the percentage could be fifty-fifty, if they had more cullet available.

Glass such as windows, light bulbs, and mirrors isn't easily disposed of. New York City and Baltimore mix these "problem" glasses with asphalt and spread it on the road. This "glassphalt" uses from five to twenty percent glass. It doesn't puncture tires. It makes for better tire traction. And it costs less than using gravel for the same purpose.

Used Car Oil

Car owners know that periodically changing their auto oil is vital. But where does the old, dirty oil go? For many years it's gone down the drain, unless it was burned in industrial furnaces, polluting the air!

Now there are re-refineries. These refineries clean used motor oil for reuse. Safety-Kleen, one such company, has plants in Illinois, Indiana, and Ontario.

Ashes

As you already know, ash left over from burning trash becomes trash itself. And even when it's not toxic, it's a big headache.

Marion County, Oregon, made cash from ash.

Getting rid of oil is a problem.

In 1989 they diluted it with water and sprayed it through an irrigation system as fertilizer for a crop of oats. A bumper crop of oats sprang up. It became hay for animal bedding and land erosion control.

Burning coal for electricity makes a lot of fly ash. Who needs fly ash? The American Electric Power Service Corp. has come up with thirty-two ash-to-cash uses. It can replace talc in outdoor paints. It can be part of a type of plastic used for auto dashboards, screwdriver handles, patio furniture, and football helmets. Fly ash mixed with water can be laid under concrete or asphalt as road fill. Ash mixed with salt can be used for snow and ice control on roads.

Collecting Recyclables

Collier County, Florida, actually mines its local landfill for recyclables! Mining equipment scoops out garbage and puts it on a conveyor belt. (Large items like, say, a stove, are put aside and dealt with separately.)

The garbage on the conveyor belt is shaken over mesh with 2½-inch openings. This gets rid of stuff that has already decomposed into compost. The rest is separated into metals, plastics, rubber, glass, and wood. Then these materials are sold to recycling centers.

The landfill is left with room for less recyclable garbage. The compost that came through the mesh is used to cover that garbage.

Indianapolis, Indiana's, nonprofit Cash for Trash program doesn't mine garbage, but it'll buy it! Citizens sell glass containers, plastic liter bottles, and aluminum and steel cans to any of ten centers. Because of this program, six million pounds of 1990 garbage did *not* go to landfills. And consumers made $745,936!

Sometimes waste management companies cut out the middleman and open buy-back sites for ordinary people to bring recyclables. Companies such as Alcoa Recycling and Reynolds Aluminum Recycling take aluminum cans, of course. But did you know that they also take other metal products such as old aluminum baseball bats and lawn furniture, bent-up pots and pans, and even items made out of copper and brass?

*Check for this symbol when you go shopping.
It's the official recycling logo.*

A lot of old refrigerators give up the ghost and
are junked. But they contain CFC's (chlorofluoro-
carbons) that snack on the earth's ozone layer
when let into the air.

The Appliance Recycling Center will come to the
rescue. They have an evacuation system to get the
CFC's out of the fridge, but keep them out of the
air. The ozone is safe. The rest of the fridge can
be recyclable scrap metal. And the evacuated
CFC's? They're reused in another refrigerator!

7
Cleaning Up in the Garbage Biz

Garbage is expensive. It costs money to buy land for landfills and to buy sanitation trucks and hire pickup crews. Then, the average cost of local land-fill dumping can be eight to ten dollars per ton. But when local trash must be taken out of state, the cost can go to two hundred dollars a ton.

It costs money to run an incinerator to burn trash. Keeping the incinerater in top condition costs money every year. Sewage plants cost money. When accidents happen, cleanups cost money. Not even recycling comes cheap. Pickup, processing, making new products, and research cost hard, cold cash.

Who can afford all this? Not mom-and-pop junk-yards. Waste management companies are taking over! Managing waste may be the growth industry of the 1990s!

Managing waste is becoming increasingly more sophisticated in the nineties!

These companies build and maintain landfills, clean incinerator filters and smokestacks, send consultants to help companies dispose of waste efficiently, clean accidental leakages and spills, and provide such folks as "environmental engineers," and "trash industry analysts!"

The "Kings of the Garbage Heap" are Waste Management, Browning-Ferris Industries, Laidlaw Waste Systems (based in Toronto), Attwoods, Western Waste Industries (based in California), and Chambers Development (based in Pennsylvania), just to name a few. Make no mistake. They are cleaning up in the garbage business. Waste

Management's 1987 Annual Report showed that they made $2,757,000,000 that year!

These companies will take away any trash you want gone — for a price. They handle hazardous as well as nonhazardous waste. They will even destroy illegal drugs confiscated by the government. They look for new dump sites, and can afford to build them to EPA standards. They can afford the best in incineration. They are even finding gold in trash-to-energy projects and recycling.

Some types of waste handling are becoming big news. Reports show that in 1990, 345 million tons of hazardous waste were created. Chemicals made up half the problem. Other materials included metals, petroleum, and coal products. Every year more substances are being declared hazardous. Managing this waste, an industry that hardly existed fifteen years ago, is growing by leaps and bounds. Experts predict that $173.5 billion dollars should be tied up in hazardous waste management by 1995.

Besides managing today's waste, hazardous waste management services handle old landfills where dangerous substances are leaching into surrounding soils. They clean up after ruptured oil tankers, leaky waste pipes, asbestos-laced buildings, and old dump sites full of any number of noxious chemicals coming out of rusty barrels.

In 1980 waste management companies hit the jackpot. A federal Environmental Protection Agency (EPA) program came into effect, known as Superfund. A $1.6 billion fund was set aside for finding and cleaning up some of the United States' worst waste sites.

The EPA figured there couldn't be *that* many sites, so instead of taking on the job themselves, the money would be used to hire independent cleanup firms. The plan was to find the sites, clean them, locate the original owners, and make them pay back the costs.

Surprise! Instead of several hundred sites — several thousand popped (or, bubbled) up! Everybody wanted a piece of the polluted pie.

By 1985, Superfund was refunded for $8.5 billion until 1990. At the moment, estimates for future cleanups are around $300 billion. Waste management companies are happy to help — and soak up the bucks.

What about the original plan to have guilty dumpsters pay up? Sometimes the companies originally guilty are long gone. And even when they're not, they don't want to pay. So more money is spent on lawsuits!

Sometimes the EPA sues corporations that had their toxic wastes quietly dumped in illegal or substandard landfills. Or they sue the owners of the landfills that took the waste. Sometimes they even sue the cities the landfills were in, if those cities knew what was going on.

Sometimes while the EPA sues the corporations, the corporations sue municipal or county agencies. After all, they may have given their hazardous waste over to a municipal garbage facility in good faith. Then that garbage might have been trucked to a substandard landfill for thirty or forty years.

Sadly, just as there are dishonest business people — there are dishonest waste management companies. In 1992, EPA officials found two illegal dump sites in Louisiana. They were only two of thousands nationwide. And they were small potatoes. Still, hundreds of barrels of chemicals, hospital waste, lab waste, and experimental pesticides had to be cleaned up.

On one of the sites, a waste management company truck was found, and a trailer from the same company was found on the other site. The trailer was crammed with seventy-five drums of corrosives, flammable solids, and flammable liquids.

It's very important for waste management companies to deal properly with hazardous substances such as the chemicals in these car batteries.

Institutions who thought they'd hired someone to safely dispose of dangerous substances were shocked. Many drums had been picked up at universities outside of Louisiana. Officials of those universities came out with records to try and figure out which barrels ended up where.

Once again, this all cost money. Universities had paid the dishonest hauling company. Finding the illegal sites cost money. The discovery, investigation, and cleanup cost money.

Money spent, money earned — it all goes around and around in a circle of green, propelled by garbage!

8
Garbage Around the World

Western Nations

Canadians throw away more per person than any other country — almost four pounds per day per person! By comparison, Americans and Australians are next with 3.5 pounds per person per day. West Germans run a close third with three pounds.

Canadians are taking their garbage problem seriously. Starting with marketers, Canadians are aiming at reducing by fifty percent the amount of stuff their goods are wrapped in by the year 2000. They also recycle aggressively. Many Canadian offices have two wastepaper baskets — one for recyclable paper and one for regular trash. Recycling firms pick up the usable paper at no charge. In fact, as one corporate exec said, "The company even pays *us* a couple of thousand dollars a month."

Many Canadian soft drink containers are refillable. In fact, *all* of Prince Edward Island's soft-drink containers are refillable. Shoppers are encouraged to bring their own reusable shopping sacks to stores, to buy more items in bulk, and to have appliances repaired instead of throwing them away and getting new ones.

One of Canada's largest supermarket chains (Loblaw Companies) has come up with its own line of environmentally friendly products. These products include everything from shopping bags and detergents to coffee filters. Marketing studies show that shoppers choose "President's Choice Green" brand products over others.

Some Canadian companies have discovered that old ways may have been best. In 1985 Vancouver's Avalon Dairy, Ltd. went back to delivering milk exclusively in refillable glass bottles rather than in throwaway containers.

As of 1990, Britain was still dumping ninety percent of its refuse in landfills. But in 1989, landfill standards were raised, making the maintenance more expensive. Cheap local dumps are running out of room, so more and more of Britain's trash must be transported to ever-more-distant areas. This transport costs money.

Instead of recycling, Britain leans more toward using waste material for energy. At reclamation centers, garbage is sorted. As garbage passes through a revolving barrel, small bits fall through a mesh. A magnet removes some metals.

What's left is newpaper, cardboard, plastics, and wood, textiles, leather, and some metal. This mix is compacted, dried, and made into "fuel pellets." Burned instead of coal, these pellets generate heat, power, and electricity from garbage. A big problem is that many British incinerators must be updated so that harmful gases will not pass into the atmosphere.

Though composting isn't a big British industry yet, compost may soon start replacing peat as a soil conditioner. British peat reserves are expected to give out in about thirty years. As one researcher said, "Compost has many of the properties of peat — it is a good organic base and holds water."

Austria has outlawed putting goods in any package that cannot be recycled. One Austrian county — Neunkirchen — has been recycling or composting two thirds of its household and industrial trash as of 1990.

Apart from Great Britain, European nations compost much more trash than the United States and Canada. Munich even tested compost curb-side-pickup in 1990. Forty thousand households got a "biobin" into which they put compostable garbage. Biobins were picked up every two weeks, eliminating part of the costly separation process normal in recycling centers.

Almost all medical wastes in Switzerland and former West Germany are taken to regional incineration plants or plants that handle hazardous waste. It means that individual hospitals don't have to get rid of their own waste in the best way they can. Regional centers are kept in top condition. Workers at these plants are highly trained, both in school and also on the site.

Switzerland and Germany require pharmacies to take back leftover medicines. This way, households don't throw leftover medicines down the drain (and probably have them end up in the water supply) or live with the danger that small children could get hold of old medicines. The pharmacies collect and send the medicinal waste to incinerators.

Former West Germany has an environmental stamp of approval called the "Blue Angel." This stamp tells consumers which products are less harmful to the environment. The stamp comes with a short explanation: "Environmentally friendly because . . ." and then, why the product got the stamp. It may be made of recycled material, or have a very low emissions rate, or it may use no asbestos.

The Orient

Japan doesn't have room for a lot of solid waste. There is literally nowhere to put it, so they must meet the problem head-on or live in it!

The Japanese generate only about 2.2 pounds of garbage per person per day. Half of home and industrial wastes are recycled. Over half of what's left is incinerated to ash. Only ashes and unrecyclable garbage goes to landfill — that's about fif-

The "Blue Angel" is former West Germany's environmental stamp of approval.

teen percent of the original garbage. About two percent of Japan's garbage is composted.

Trash burned in state-of-the-art incinerators helps provide heat and electricity for parts of Tokyo. Incinerators are privately owned and operated, but the government provides anywhere from twenty-five to fifty percent of the initial building cost, to make sure that it's done right. The incinerators are tested every two months to make sure their emissions are within safety standards. Their workers are specially trained.

Japan's excellent recycling stems from the fact that almost all their raw materials — most wood and chemicals, and all of its fossil fuels — must be imported. So the more they can reuse, the better.

Private dealers and volunteer groups pick up recycled goods. Japan recycles half its paper. Two thirds of its bottles are reused at least three times. Some bottles are reused up to twenty times! Almost half of all metal cans are recycled as well.

Japan has something called an "EcoMark" label. This goes on products that are good for the environment. Compost bins, for example, get an EcoMark. So do kitchen sink traps and recyclable bottles.

Chinese villagers recycle almost everything! They go far beyond what most folks in other countries would do. Old wrapping paper and newspapers become toilet paper. Old magazines become textbook covers or wallpaper. Chinese children make toys of cloth scraps.

When villagers shop, they take not only their own shopping bags, but their own bottles. A single oil bottle will be filled many, many times over several years. And the same plastic bag will be filled over and over with laundry detergent.

Village homes combine the kitchen with the bedroom, so that the cooking facilities heat up the sleeping room. Village pigs and chickens live on scraps. They provide manure for fertilizer, and can become food themselves. Chickens provide eggs. Unlike other countries, Chinese villagers use human as well as animal manure for fertilizer.

Eastern Europe

East European countries have paid a price for being under Soviet domination. Socialist countries worshipped industry. They wanted big factories with big output. But this made big garbage, chemical byproducts, and toxic pollution.

Years of workers' complaints were ignored. A worker in a huge former East German film factory tried to bring company records of illnesses due to chemical exposure to government attention in the 1980s. "We were told," he said, "almost immediately to destroy all the copies. . . . Everything was produce, produce, produce — and to heck with the rest."

Former East Germany was one of the most polluted countries in Europe. For decades it was the center of chemical works, and huge open-pit coal mines. There were no restrictions on air control or soil and water contamination.

After German reunification, ninety toxic dumps were discovered in eastern Germany. Said one former East German, "There are probably hundreds of others. No one knows for sure."

Now western Germany is putting up $700 million to help eastern Germany clean up. They hope to get reunified Germany to the same standards by the year 2000. Can it be done? Check back in the year 2000!

Since the breakup of the Soviet bloc, Western nations have been shocked at the toxic conditions of once-beautiful Eastern countries.

Two thirds of Czechoslovakia's rivers are contaminated by industrial, mining, and agricultural waste. A third of its forests are dying from air pollution, mainly because its power plants burn brown coal. Three quarters of Poland's forests are endangered by the same type of air pollution. Two thirds of its raw sewage goes into water systems untreated. Dumped industrial and agricultural waste have contaminated two thirds of Bulgaria's rivers. Overuse and improper use of pesticides have damaged much of the country's wildlife.

Clearly, Eastern Europe needs help. The World Bank loaned Poland $18 million just to study its toxic problems and come up with some solutions. Garbage and hazardous waste companies in the West would love to help — for a price. Trouble is, Eastern Europe is a bit short on cash! As one executive said, "Everybody knows the need is there. But in order to have a market, you've got to have the need and the money."

One way out is as old as humanity — barter. The deals get complicated. A cleanup company sells modern waste-to-energy equipment to an East European country. With the equipment, the East European country supplies a nearby Western country with electricity. The Western country pays — not the East Europeans for the electricity, but the cleanup company for the original energy equipment!

The East European country gets rid of trash without polluting its air. One Western country gets "free" electricity. And the cleanup company gets paid hard currency for its equipment.

The International Garbage Market —
A Dirty Business

"Thinking about making money?" a Paris newspaper ad asked. "Hazardous toxic waste a billion-dollar-a-year business. Think about this! No experience necessary. No equipment needed. No educational requirements."

In the 1940s, the world produced ten million metric tons of hazardous waste a year. That amount is now over 320 million metric tons a year, worldwide. Because of this increase, an international garbage market has sprung up. This is a market for which, as one periodical put it, "only the greedy and ruthless need apply."

Basically, waste companies from developed nations have been paying desperately poor underdeveloped countries to take in such wastes as

The Orient is a leader in recycling waste.
But as you can see from this river in Thailand,
pollution is still a problem.

acids, cyanides, pesticides, solvents, lead com-
pounds, mercury, arsenic, PCB's and dioxins, infectious hospital and laboratory waste, obsolete
explosives, herbicides and pesticides, nerve gases,
and radioactive materials.

Africa, Latin America, and the Caribbean have
been the main recipients of this trade. Africa, in
particular, has allowed itself to be the "secret
dumping ground for millions of tons of nuclear or
toxic industrial waste." Why? Lots of money.

American and European countries have been

making deals with several African nations. The deals entail money amounts like $20 million, plus economic assistance for anywhere from ten to thirty years. The "host" agrees to take anywhere from one to five million tons of toxic or nuclear waste and pretend that it's not going to hurt anybody. The going landfill rate for hazardous waste in the United States is $200 to $250 per ton. In Africa, it's $40 per ton.

According to *Africa Report* magazine, as of 1988, companies from France, Holland, Canada, America, Britain, the former Soviet Union, Norway, Switzerland, and Italy have all dealt in dumping toxic or radioactive waste in Africa for a hefty price. The Organization for African Unity has been banding together to stop more waste imports from being left in their countries. Not surprisingly, Nigeria passed a law in 1989 that gives life imprisonment to anyone caught dumping illegal hazardous waste in that country.

Africa isn't the only country being dumped on. Any country poor and desperate enough to take in nuclear waste is fair game to an unscrupulous waste trader. Waste goes to the South Pacific, Central and South America, the Pacific Rim, and it is quietly dumped in oceans.

A partial list of these goings-on, as of 1988, was printed in the *Journal of Business Ethics*. It listed only actual waste shipments and active proposals. Because of space, we can only reprint a few.

State or Country:	Waste:	Dumped in:
French government	Radioactive	Benin
Italian megafirm	Toxic liquid	Dominican Republic
British firm	Chemical waste	Equatorial Guinea
U.S.—Colorado firm	Uranium waste	Gabon
U.S.—Pennsylvania firm	Toxic ash	Guinea, Haiti
U.S.—Texas firm	PCB waste	Dominican Republic
U.S.—Texas firm	PCB waste	Mexico, South Africa
U.S.—NJ firm	Lead waste	Mexico
U.S.—NJ firm	Mercury sludge	South Africa
U.S.—Florida firm	Solvents	Paraguay, Peru
U.S.—California firm	Hazardous waste	Tonga
U.S.—general	Lead waste	Zimbabwe
U.S.—general	Lead waste	South Korea
U.S.—general	Lead waste	Nigeria
U.S.—general	Lead waste	India

Greenpeace International has been watching the global waste trade since 1986 and still is. Hopefully, this shameful market will come to an end as more people become aware of it. Some countries may be dying to get rid of their waste, but other countries shouldn't be dying when they get it.

9
What Can I Do?

You don't manage a landfill or have control over where nuclear waste goes. You can't catch illegal dumpers or stop the international garbage trade. What, you ask, can I do?

You can get down and dirty with your own garbage. Watch what you buy. Read labels — is your hair mousse propelled with fluorocarbons? Watch what you toss. Where did the last of the deodorant go? You can nag for a good cause. What happens at your folks' place of business? Where do they, or their garage, take old car oil? And you can stay informed. What are the latest ideas in recycling and laws regarding waste? What products are "greener" than others?

At School

• If your school doesn't recycle, suggest it! Get your class to plant a tree on Earth Day. Are your

Do you have a recycling program like this one in your community?

textbooks printed on recycled paper? If not, your class can write the publishers and ask them to print their textbooks on recycled paper. Publishers want to please their customers, and they don't know what people want until they're told.

• Your class can adopt a spot and keep it clean. Some classes adopt a park, part of a riverbank, or even a section of highway bank. On Saturdays they pick up trash, rake leaves, pull weeds, or put in new plants. They also put up PLEASE DON'T LITTER signs.

• If you or your class see or hear about a company that's doing something good about using less packaging, using recycled goods, or just making a good product, write to let them know that you notice.

Does this seem silly and useless? Do you think nobody will listen because you're only a kid? Wrong! To companies you are not a kid — you are a future buyer! That makes you someone they will know in the future. And it makes your opinion important.

Remember, a company will sell anything that people will buy. Degradable plastics were developed because marketing studies showed that consumers wanted them. Technology is sometimes available — but companies need demand before they will act.

• When you have art projects, use recycled products like leftover egg cartons, squares of cloth from old clothes, or the back of scrap paper. Use water-based paints and markers, instead of oil-based ones.

At Home

• The big suggestion is obvious. Don't litter. Ever. Anywhere.

• When you have a party and use helium balloons, don't let them fly off into the air. It looks pretty now, but who knows where the balloon remains will land? Remember, a balloon gobbled up by a wild animal might harm it badly.

• Don't be a drip — keep an eye on your faucets

Boy Scouts from the San Fernando Valley got together with the folks at the Reynolds Metals Company to clean up this California beach.

to make sure none is wasting water by dripping. Is your toilet leaking water? Here's how to find out. Have an adult help you take the top off the toilet tank and put ten to twelve drops of food coloring into the tank. Make sure that no one uses the toilet for the next quarter of an hour. If any of the colored water from the tank shows up in the bowl, your toilet is wasting water and should be fixed.

• Stop the flood of junk mail. Ask to be taken off the list by writing to: Direct Mail Marketing Association, 6 East 43rd Street, New York, NY 10017.

• If you garden, set aside a portion for composting. If you don't, find out if your yard waste can be taken to a composting center.

• Use items that can be washed and used again, instead of thrown away. For instance, use cloth instead of paper napkins, cloth kitchen rags and dust cloths instead of paper towels. If there's a baby in the house, suggest cloth instead of disposable diapers.

• Find out where to take home toxins, like the last bit of paint, old motor oil, dead batteries, the rest of the weed killer, leftover medicines, the empty bug spray can, and old makeup. Keep your home toxins in one safe place — (a box?) — and take them to a drop-off center for hazardous materials.

• Change your personal habits to help keep the earth cleaner. The editor of *Packaging Digest* says that change is not all up to industry — people have to change as well. This means carrying groceries in reusable shopping bags. It means buying different sizes of products than you may be used to. It means looking to see if packaging is made from partly recycled material. Buy sodas in returnable cans or bottles. Use roll-ons and pump cans instead of spray products. Use reusable instead of disposable razors.

• Use both sides of paper for letter writing and homework. Use the back of leftover computer paper for figuring out your math homework or essay outline. Or cut the paper into quarters and use it instead of buying phone message pads. When you're finished, recycle the paper.

Knowledge Is Power

Buzzworm, the environmental journal, takes its name from the Old West term for rattlesnake. The inside front cover explains: "Since a rattlesnake can be thought of as symbolizing a very effective form of communication — it buzzes and you react — we thought it an appropriate name for a publication reporting on the condition of worldwide environmental conservation." *Buzzworm* comes out every other month. It is funded through private donations, payment for putting ads in the magazine, and subscriptions. It's not part of any political or environmental organization. It's important for *Buzzworm* to be independent, since it's a watchdog on the world. Subscription rate (as of 1992) is $21 in the United States, $26 for Canada, and $31–$39 overseas (depending on whether it's surface or air mail).

For info, write to: *Buzzworm*, 2305 Canyon Boulevard, Suite 206, Boulder, CO 80302. (Tel: 303/442–1969).

Want to know what's tops in trash? Need the goods on garbage? The following bi-monthly magazine will tell all.

Garbage comes out every other month from — Brooklyn, NY. Stateside subscriptions are $21 a year. For information, write to: *Garbage*, 435 Ninth Street, Brooklyn, NY 11215-4101.

Does your small town or neighborhood want to recycle, but doesn't know quite how to start? The

Recycling Handbook for Local Government and Organizations may help. It tells how to design a whole integrated program — involving communities in the effort, picking up stuff, where to take it, and what to do with it once you've got it. It includes case studies of already started programs. It also has cost estimates. If your town doesn't recycle, maybe the mayor could use a copy of this booklet!

For information, write: Innovation Groups, Inc., P.O. Box 16645, Tampa, FL 33687-6645.

Another recycling guide for small towns is called *Why Waste a Second Chance?* Put out by the National Association of Towns and Townships, the booklet sells for $11.

For information, write to: NATAT, 1522 K Street, NW, Suite 600, Washington, DC 20005.

For information about vinyl plastic recycling, contact: The Vinyl Institute, Wayne Interchange Plaza II, 155 Route 46W, Wayne, NJ 07470.

Some good places to write for information about solid waste disposal and recycling are:

Keep America Beautiful, Inc., Mill River Plaza, 9 West Broad Street, Stamford, CT 06902.
Council for Solid Waste Solutions at 1275 K Street NW, Washington, DC 20005.
Waste Watch Center, 16 Haverhill Street, Andover, MA 01810.

National Solid Waste Management Association, 1730 Rhode Island Avenue NW, Washington, DC 20036.

A Peek at the Future

Morning. Well, you've slept in a bit since it's a weekend. You turn on a light and get up. The light may be fluorescent, halogen, or sodium. Yours is a compact fluorescent bulb. It uses about one fourth as much energy as the old incandescent type, and seems to last forever.

It doesn't, of course. When it burns out, you'll take it back to the light fixture store when you buy a new bulb. Old bulbs are picked up by the bulb manufacturer. They're crushed in an airtight container, and the gases inside are reclaimed. New bulbs are made from the old.

You pour some cereal from a box made of recycled newspaper. As you munch down breakfast you read your morning paper, which is fifty percent recycled material. The newsprint ink is a soybean-based product.

One article is about the cleanup of an old hazardous-waste site. The cleanup crew used "glassification" to clean the mess. Electricity run into the soil turned contaminants into a glasslike substance. Then the soil was cleaned.

Outside, you see the diaper service truck going past your house. Must be diaper day at the Smiths'. You finish the paper and toss it into the "paper" bin. It's next to the glass, metal, plastic, and organic bins. Hmm. The organic bin looks pretty full. Time to empty it into the composter. Glass and metal pickup is Tuesday. Paper and plastic day is Thursday. Last Tuesday you forgot about pickup, and your bins were full. What a pain! You had to drive your stuff to a drop-off yourself.

You drive your car to the store. The car is made almost entirely of recycled plastic. You need quite a few things, so you brought four large shopping totes. In one is your refillable milk jug.

Your car is getting low on fuel, so you go to a gas station and fill up with ethanol. Ethanol is made from grain. You've been thinking, though, about getting a new car. Maybe this time, a solar-powered electric car. Or maybe one that runs on hydrogen.

You check your mail. An electric bill. Hmm, not too bad considering what these bills used to be. Electricity is a lot cheaper since the waste-to-energy plants became so efficient. Plants also run on solar power in areas where this is practical, and the windy Great Plains' plants use windmills. Of course, the solar panels on the south side of your house's roof help a lot. It took a while to pay for those, but they've earned it back.

It's the weekend, so you can do a bit of gardening. You get your tools from a toolshed of cinder blocks made from incinerator ash. Your neighbor has one made of recycled plastic lumber. Looks just like the real thing, only it doesn't warp.

Doing a bit of housecleaning, you take out a cleaner and pump-spray it on a counter. The cleaner is made from citrus. You wipe it off the counter with a kitchen rag and then rinse the rag out. Can't vacuum today, because the old vac gave up the ghost and is in the shop being fitted for a new motor.

It's a nice day. You can remember the bad old days when the skies weren't this nice. You've tried to explain smog to the kids, but they don't really understand.

They're at the park today. You can remember when that park was a stinking garbage heap. It was mined for reusables about ten years ago, covered with garbage-composted soil, and made into a park. There are a lot of these parks and public lands now.

It's almost warm enough for a trip to the beach. This is something you especially look forward to. When you were a kid, nobody was allowed to swim on that beach. The sand was full of litter — broken glass, paper, plastic bags, and soda cans. And the water was too polluted with oil slicks and chemical spills to let anyone near it.

Litter laws are strict nowadays. And even if someone gets away with it, the plastics at least are sun-degradable and melt away eventually. It took a long time and a lot of tax dollars to clean up the water, but it was worth it. Now that fossil fuels aren't used much, there's not as much oil to spill!

But you're even more excited about what your children will probably grow up with — fusion. Scientists are getting mighty close to making it practical. It's the same power that fuels the sun. It's cheap, infinitely renewable, and doesn't leave harmful waste all over like the nuclear power plants you can still recall. Fusion will actually generate more energy than it takes to make it!

In *their* future, energy will be so cheap, they'll pay that electric bill with pennies! Streets and sidewalks will be heated underneath to melt snow, because that will be cheaper than salt or de-icer! Farms could even open up in Antarctica!

Lucky them. Lucky you. Lucky Earth.

10
Trashy Trivia

A.J. Weberman became famous — sort of — in the late 1960s by collecting trash of the stars. He said people would be surprised what he found out by looking through famous folks' trash bins. He knew what they ate, what they read, and how many kids and cats and dogs they had, and even read unfinished letters. Singer Bob Dylan got so upset at this invasion of his privacy that he hired a guard to keep A.J. out of his trash!

It's here — edible packaging! Food scientists have come up with a cellulose coating that laminates food like plastic. The Drumstick Co. of Columbus, Ohio, is using the new product in their drumstick ice cream cones. They coat the inside so ice cream moisture doesn't make the cone soggy!

This isn't the only wrapping available. Another is made from *chitosan*, a substance found in shrimp and lobster shells. It's not something some countries would want to wolf down. But other, more fish reliant countries such as Japan and Norway don't mind.

Unless you've been living under a rock, you've probably noticed a change in cartoon heroes and villains. Cartoons have gotten "greener." Superman and Batman battled bad guys. Other superheroes specialized in keeping Earth safe from invading aliens. But superheroes like Captain Planet and the Planeteers and the Teenage Mutant Ninja Turtles are most likely battling "eco-villains" — villains who do bad things to the environment.

"Turtle Tips" has kids as young as four or five refusing to eat hamburgers wrapped in anything but paper. And Captain Planet's "You Have the Power" motto encourages viewers to realize that environmental improvement starts at home.

In 1990 some school students were treated to "Dr. T" — a "trashologist." Otherwise known as the "Rajah of Rubbish," Dr. T taught grade- and middle-schoolers about landfills, hazardous waste, and recycling. He called his program of rap music, juggling, and magic "Garbage Is My Bag."

Glendale, Arizona, officials decided to make recycling fun, and a little strange. The fun part is

CAPTAIN PLANET
AND THE PLANETEERS

(l-r) GI - *WATER*, KWAME - *EARTH*, WHEELER - *FIRE*, MA-TI - *HEART*, LINKA - *WIND*

*Captain Planet teams up with the
Planeteers to save Earth!*

"feeding" the drop-off bins — brightly colored "ig-loos" with faces. The strange part is "Recycleman," complete with superhero outfit! His shirtfront sports a recycling symbol, and his cape looks like recycled newsprint! Recycleman drops into schools every so often, to pump up recycling efforts.

Researchers at the State University of New York at Stony Brook has developed a cinder block made from sixty-seven percent incinerator ash. Put together with "sand aggregate," these blocks are actually stronger than regular cinder block! In 1991 they built a boathouse out of the trashy blocks. They're monitoring air quality and durability of the blocks over the next several years. If everything checks out, we may not be living on top of our garbage anymore — we'll be living *in* it!

Asian and Indian countries have found that cut-up tires make excellent sandal bottoms. They're cheap, durable — and hug the road!

A store called *Used Rubber, USA* in San Francisco has another use for old tires. They take the inner tubes and make items such as purses, pouches, knapsacks, and motor- or bicycle saddlebags from them. The company also makes belts, sandals, and — clothing!

Yes, you can have a skirt, jumper, or pants made of pure Goodyear! Designs vary, but woven strips of rubber make a very nice effect.

Do you think Darell suspects that his Goodyear tire may one day be a jumper?

All tread threads are waterproof, stainproof, and incredibly durable. Biggest sellers are brand-name handbags — only the brand names are Firestone, Michelin, and Pirelli! All products come with a lifetime guarantee. And if anything gets damaged the owners say, "You can always bring it in for an overhaul."

Who invented the first "biological" car? Henry Ford — and he did it in 1941. The car's body was made of plastic made from soybeans. It rolled on tires made from goldenrod. It ran on ethanol, a fuel made from corn. Why didn't it sell? Because oil was cheaper than ethanol after World War II.

Henry Ford was ahead of his time when he invented the first "biological car."

In ancient Athens, the penalty for polluting the city water supply was death.

Water facts:
- 4.8 billion gallons of water are flushed every day in the United States.
- 22,627 square miles of toilet tissue are used every day in the United States.
- 7.7 metric tons of sewage sludge is generated every year in the United States.
- Household wastewater is:
  - 33 percent flushed
  - 26 percent used for washing clothes
  - 19.6 percent used for bathing
  - 11.3 percent down the kitchen sink
  - 2.5 percent used in automatic dishwashers
  - 1.8 percent used in garbage disposals
  - The rest — miscellaneous